World of Reading 2

Paint This Town Red

Adapted by **Steve Behling**
Based on ***Descendants: The Rise of Red***
by **Dan Frey & Russell Sommer**

Disney PRESS
LOS ANGELES • NEW YORK

Welcome back to Auradon Prep!
Uma is now the principal.
She and Fairy Godmother send
an invitation to a new student.

Who’s that new student? you wonder.
Well, wonder no more!
Her name is Red.
She lives in Wonderland.

Red's mom is the Queen of Hearts. She's hard to get along with. Lucky for Red, she has a friend, named Maddox.

Maddox shows Red his new invention.
It can take someone back in time
and give them what they want most.
Red takes it.

Meanwhile, in another land, Cinderella and King Charming get ready to send their daughter, Chloe, to Auradon Prep.

Before Chloe leaves for school,
Cinderella gives her a pair
of glass shoes.
They're just like Cinderella's.

Back in Wonderland,
the Queen of Hearts wants
Red to be mean, just like her.
But Red wants to live her own life!

Red gets Uma's invitation.
To her surprise,
the Queen says Red can go!
The Queen drives Red to school.

Chloe and Red arrive.
Chloe learns that her mom and the Queen used to be friends!
But something happened that made the Queen turn evil.

The Queen opens her Looking Glass.
It can see the future.
She shows it to Red.

Red sees herself,
seated on a throne next to her mom.
Red looks just as evil
as the Queen of Hearts!

Fairy Godmother and Uma
welcome the new students.
But the Queen of Hearts interrupts.
She's taking over Auradon!

Red doesn't like her mom's plan. She wants her mom to be proud of her, but she knows this isn't right.

Red has to stop her.
She decides to use the time machine!
But Chloe thinks Red is evil, too,
so she tries to interrupt.

Red and Chloe go back in time!
"Where are we?" Chloe wonders.
"Not where," Red says. "When!"

Chloe and Red see someone
who looks like Fairy Godmother.
It *is* Fairy Godmother,
but she is just a kid!

Chloe and Red have gone back to when Auradon Prep was called Merlin Academy. Merlin thinks Chloe and Red are new students!

Red meets her mom's younger self.
Her name is Bridget,
and she's really nice!

They even meet Chloe's mom, Ella, and her dad, Prince Charming!

Bridget is friendly to everyone. She has made cupcakes to share with the students. But not everyone wants to be friends.

This young pirate with a hook
for a hand does not!
He sneers at Chloe and her friends.
He's a Villain Kid,
and he's not the only one!

Uliana is the leader of the VKs.
She is mean to everyone,
especially Bridget.

Maybe Uliana is the one
who makes Bridget turn evil?
Red and Chloe visit Ella for help.
They meet Ella's wicked stepmother.

Ella says that the Villain Kids hang out at the Black Lagoon. They'll find Uliana there.

In the Black Lagoon,
Red and Chloe sneak up on Uliana.
Uliana plans to play
a mean trick on Bridget!

And to do it, she's going to steal a magic book from Merlin's office. Chloe and Red leave, but some angry eels attack! Red saves Chloe.

Red tells Chloe they need
to steal the book first.
But Chloe doesn't want
to break the rules.
She asks Ella for advice.

Thanks to Ella,
Chloe makes up her mind
to help Red get the magic book.

But the Villain Kids are coming! Morgie keeps watch in a tree while Uliana and the others enter Merlin's office.

Chloe and Red find the book.
But Uliana takes it from them!
When she tries to open it,
a spell freezes her in place!

Chloe and Red get the book back.
They stopped the prank on Bridget!
Chloe and Red can go home.
They hope everything has changed—
for the better.